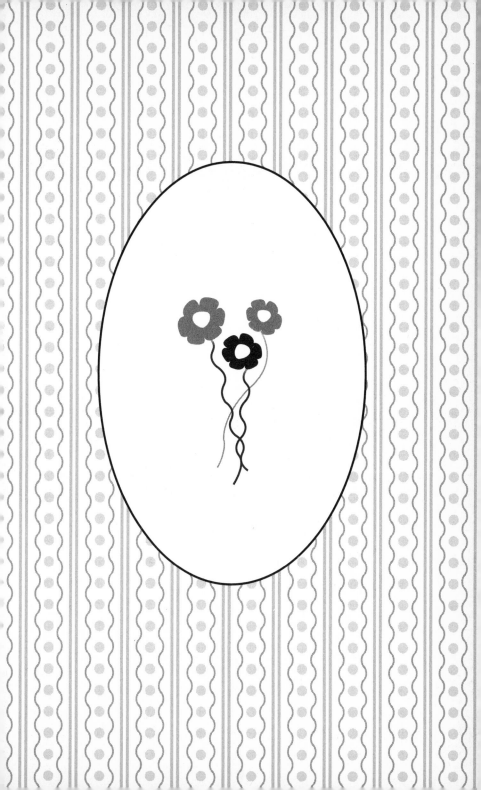

PRINCESS P🌸SEY
and the
NEW FIRST GRADER

Stephanie Greene

ILLUSTRATED BY

Stephanie Roth Sisson

G. P. PUTNAM'S SONS

AN IMPRINT OF PENGUIN GROUP (USA) INC.

Don't miss

the other Princess Posey books

For the Cookies.

—S.G.

For Betsy Shaffer,
the perfect teacher at the perfect time.
Thank you for all you do
for children—lucky kids!
—S.R.S.

G. P. PUTNAM'S SONS
An imprint of Penguin Young Readers Group.
Published by The Penguin Group.
Penguin Group (USA) Inc., 375 Hudson Street, New York, NY 10014, USA.
Penguin Group (Canada), 90 Eglinton Avenue East, Suite 700, Toronto, Ontario M4P
2Y3, Canada (a division of Pearson Penguin Canada Inc.).
Penguin Books Ltd, 80 Strand, London WC2R 0RL, England.
Penguin Ireland, 25 St. Stephen's Green, Dublin 2, Ireland
(a division of Penguin Books Ltd).
Penguin Group (Australia), 707 Collins Street, Melbourne, Victoria 3008, Australia
(a division of Pearson Australia Group Pty Ltd).
Penguin Books India Pvt Ltd, 11 Community Centre,
Panchsheel Park, New Delhi–110 017, India.
Penguin Group (NZ), 67 Apollo Drive, Rosedale, Auckland 0632, New Zealand
(a division of Pearson New Zealand Ltd).
Penguin Books South Africa, Rosebank Office Park, 181 Jan Smuts Avenue,
Parktown North 2193, South Africa.
Penguin China, B7 Jiaming Center, 27 East Third Ring Road North,
Chaoyang District, Beijing 100020, China.
Penguin Books Ltd, Registered Offices: 80 Strand, London WC2R 0RL, England.

Library of Congress Cataloging-in-Publication Data
Greene, Stephanie. Princess Posey and the new first grader / Stephanie Greene ;
illustrated by Stephanie Roth Sisson.   p. cm.—(Princess Posey ; bk. 6)
Summary: "When Posey's first grade class gets a new student, she worries her
friends will like the new girl more than her."—Provided by publisher.
[1. Best friends—Fiction. 2. Friendship—Fiction. 3. Jealousy—Fiction.
4. Schools—Fiction.] I. Sisson, Stephanie Roth, ill. II. Title.
PZ7.G8434Ppt 2013   [E]—dc23   2012029771
ISBN 978-0-399-25712-4
1 3 5 7 9 10 8 6 4 2

CONTENTS

THREE PEAS
IN A POD

"What's this word, Mom?" Posey asked. She pointed to a word in her book.

Her mom was making dinner. She came over and looked.

"It's *added*," her mom said. "To add something."

"*Then he added a splash of mud,*"
Posey read. She laughed. "This is
such a silly story."

"You're doing very well with it,"
said her mom.

"I love reading," said Posey. "I'm
going to read so much, I'll get into
the blue group."

Reading was very important in
first grade. The top group was blue.
They read books with blue dots on
them.

The next group was red. Posey
was in the red group with Ava and

Nikki. They read books with red dots on them.

After red came the yellow group. And then the green group.

The green group was at the bottom. No one wanted to read books with the green dots on them.

"All that matters is that you do the best you can," her mom said.

Posey's mom always said that. She didn't know first grade. In first grade, everyone wanted to be in the blue group.

Every month, Miss Lee assigned new reading partners. She put people together from different groups. It was so much fun to read with a partner.

"I wish Ava and Nikki could both be my reading partners," said Posey.

"Reading partners means two, doesn't it?" said her mom.

"No fair," said Posey.

Her mom laughed. "You girls are like three peas in a pod," she said.

Three peas in a pod. Posey liked that.

"I'm finished with my home-work," she said. "Can I go see Hero?"

"Sure," said her mom. "I will call you when dinner's ready."

THE MAGIC LAND GAME

Posey ran up to her room. She put on her pink tutu and her veil with the stars.

Princess Posey was ready.

She ran down the stairs and skipped to the red house next door.

"Hi, Mrs. Romero," she called. "Hi, Hero."

Mrs. Romero was planting flowers in her garden. Hero was chewing a ball next to her.

When he saw Posey, he jumped up and ran to her. He licked her face.

"You silly dog," Posey said. She scratched behind his ears.

"I think Hero likes you more than he likes peanut butter," said Mrs. Romero.

Posey laughed. Peanut butter was Hero's favorite treat.

"Can Hero play a game with me?" Posey said.

"That would be great," said Mrs. Romero. "He keeps eating my flowers."

"Come on, Hero," said Posey.

She looked around for a good place to play her new game. She called it Magic Land. She made it up herself.

"I'm the princess," Posey told Hero. "You can be my pet lion."

Hero wagged his tail.

The princess lived in a castle in the forest, Posey explained. There was a magic unicorn. It lived in an invisible cave.

"A mean giant wants to steal the unicorn," Posey said. "You and I have to protect it."

Hero looked brave.

"Come on!" Posey shouted. "Let's play!"

There was a tree stump in one corner of the yard. It could be

her pretend
castle. Posey
climbed on top.
She acted like
she was
looking

out the window at the forest.

"The giant's coming!" she cried.
"We have to save the unicorn!"

Posey jumped off the stump and
ran around the
yard. Hero ran
with her. He
jumped up and
barked.

Posey pretended the giant was getting closer and closer. Its footsteps sounded like thunder.

"Hurry, lion!" Posey shouted. "Inside the cave!"

Posey crawled into the bushes. Hero crawled in beside her. The magic unicorn was shivering. It was so afraid.

The princess patted its silver hair to calm it down.

"Shh-h-h-h," the princess warned in a soft voice.

The giant roared and stomped. The walls of the cave shook.

Posey's heart beat very fast. It felt so real!

What if the giant found them? What would it do?

But it couldn't see the invisible cave. It roared one last time and ran away.

They were safe!

Posey and Hero crawled back into the yard.

Posey could hardly wait for tomorrow. Playing her magic game with Ava and Nikki would be so much fun.

She would tell them about it at school, first thing!

THE NEW GIRL

Posey didn't get
to tell Ava and
Nikki about
Magic Land
first thing.

As soon as she got to Miss Lee's room, they rushed up to her. They had their own exciting news.

"We have a new girl," Nikki said.

"That's her," said Ava. She pointed.

A girl Posey had never seen before was holding Miss Lee's hand. They were looking at the art wall. The girl was dressed all in yellow.

Her skirt with rows and rows of
ruffles was yellow.

Her sparkly top was yellow.

Even the headband in her long
black hair was yellow.

"She looks like a real princess,"
Nikki said.

"She has real princess hair," said
Ava.

They already liked her. Posey
could tell. It gave her a funny
feeling in her stomach.

Posey put her things in her
cubby and sat down. Miss Lee and

the new girl walked to Posey's table.

"This is where you will sit," Miss Lee said. She patted the chair next to Posey. "Posey, this is Grace. I told her you would show her how we do things in our class."

Grace sat down. Miss Lee went to her desk.

Up close, Grace's headband sparkled. Her black hair was shiny.

"You want to know something amazing?" Grace said.

"What?" said Posey.

"I lost a tooth." Grace showed Posey her teeth. There was a space on top.

Posey wished she had lost a tooth.

"I love yellow," Grace said. "What color do you love?"

"Pink," said Posey.

"I bet you love it so much, you wish you had pink hair." Grace giggled.

Posey frowned. "No one has pink hair," she said.

"You can if we make up an amazing magic game," said Grace.

Posey had her own magic game. She didn't want to tell Grace about it. Or play it with her, either.

Posey's game could have only one princess.

Grace's long princess hair made Posey's stomach hurt.

STUCK LIKE GLUE

It was Grace, Grace, Grace all day. She asked Posey a million questions.

She thought everything was so amazing.

Posey didn't get to tell Ava and Nikki about her game.

"How was school?" her mom said when Posey got in the car.

"Bad." Posey buckled her seat belt.

Danny was asleep in his car seat. He was making snuffling noises.

"Danny's snoring," Posey said.

"He has a cold, the poor baby," said her mom.

"He's breathing his germs all over." Posey pinched her nose shut.

"Someone's a little grouchy this afternoon," her mom said. "Did something happen?"

"We have a new girl," said Posey. The ends of her mouth turned down. "All she wears is yellow."

"Yellow is a pretty color," her mom said. "What's her name?"

"Grace." Posey frowned. "Miss Lee made her sit next to me. She sticked to me like glue all day."

"You mean she *stuck* to you like glue." Her mom laughed. "I bet she was scared. It's hard to be new."

Posey crossed her arms over her chest.

"Why can't I have long hair?" she said.

"We tried that last summer, remember?" Her mom turned the car onto their street. "Your hair got all tangled. I had to cut out the knots."

Posey did remember. It hurt when her mom brushed it.

Her mom stopped the car in front of their garage.

"Maybe Miss Lee thinks you

and Grace will be friends," her mom said. "It might be fun to have a new friend."

Posey didn't want a new friend.

She only wanted Ava and Nikki.

"I'M A FROG, TOO!"

The next morning, Danny spilled his cereal. Posey's mom had to change his clothes.

Posey worried she would be late. But when she got to Miss Lee's room, Ava and Nikki were still in the reading corner.

Now Posey could tell them
about her game!
She started to skip.
Then she stopped.

Grace was in the reading corner, too. She was sitting on the red and blue pillow with Ava. It was the pillow Posey and Ava always shared.

"We're playing school," Nikki told Posey. "I'm the teacher."

"We're having reading time," Grace said. "I'm in the red group, too."

"Did Miss Lee say that?" said Posey.

"I'm a good reader," said Grace. "Look how fast I am!"

She held her book in front of her face. She shook her head back and forth like she was reading fast. "*A-B-C, A-B-C, A-B-C,*" she said.

Ava and Nikki laughed.

"You can read with us," Grace said to Posey.

Posey frowned. Grace acted like she knew everything.

"I don't want to," Posey said. She went to her table and sat down.

Posey worked hard all morning. When Grace tried to whisper to her, Posey said, "I'm trying to do my work."

As soon as it was recess, Posey ran to Nikki and Ava. She grabbed their hands.

"Come on!" Posey said. "Let's play the hopping game!"

The three friends ran outside. They crouched down and put their arms around their knees.

Then they jumped up high. Like springs.

Up and down. Up and down. They tried to see who could jump the highest.

"Look, I'm a frog!" Posey shouted.

"I'm a frog, too," called a voice.

Grace crouched down next to

Posey. "Let's you and me hold hands and hop," she said.

"Frogs don't have hands," said Posey.

Grace hopped to the left. Then she hopped to the right. This time, she made a funny croaking noise. She sounded just like a frog.

Posey stood up. "That's not how you do it," she said.

Ava and Nikki started to make croaking noises, too. They hopped with Grace across the grass.

Posey watched them go.

They were having so much fun.
They didn't look like they
missed Posey at all. Posey's mouth
got trembly.

What if Ava and Nikki liked
Grace more than her?

"SHE WON'T BE MY FRIEND!"

Posey went
to find Miss Lee.
She was sitting at
the picnic table.

"My stomach hurts," said
Posey.

"Sit with me." Miss Lee patted
the bench next to her. "It's almost
time to go in."

Miss Lee held Posey's hand when the class walked back to the room.

"Do you feel better now?" Miss Lee asked.

Posey nodded. She went to her cubby and put away her jacket.

Grace was putting her sweater in her cubby.

"That was so much fun," Grace said. "Ava and Nikki are my friends."

"They were my friends first," said Posey. Her eyes felt prickly. She blinked fast.

"You want to know something amazing?" Grace said. "You have a cow lips."

"I do not have cow lips," said Posey.

"I do, too," said Grace.

"I don't have cow lips!" Posey shouted. "I'm telling!"

She ran to Miss Lee's desk.

"Miss Lee! Miss Lee!" Posey cried. "Grace is calling me names!"

Grace was right behind her.

"Sorry!" Grace cried. "I said I was sorry!"

"What's going on?" said Miss Lee. "Calm down, both of you."

Posey stood still. She pressed her lips together.

"Grace," Miss Lee said quietly. "Did you call Posey a name?"

"I didn't mean to," said Grace. She sounded like she was going to cry.

"She did too," said Posey. "She hurt my feelings."

"She won't hold my hand."

Grace's face crumpled. "She won't be my friend!"

"You made croaking noises," Posey said. "That's not how you play the hopping game."

Grace started to cry.

Posey did, too.

"Oh, dear," said Miss Lee. She reached for her box of Kleenex.

CHAPTER
SEVEN

COWS WEARING LIPSTICK

It made Posey feel better to wipe her face with Miss Lee's own Kleenex. It smelled like perfume.

"Now. One at a time," said Miss Lee. "Grace, what did you say to Posey?"

"I said she had a cow lips." Grace sniffed. "I have a cow lips, too."

"Cow lips?" said Miss Lee. "I don't understand. What are cow lips?"

"This is a cow lips." Grace put her finger on the back of her head. There was a little circle where her hair stood up.

"Oh-h-h-h," Miss Lee said. She laughed her understanding laugh. "You mean a cowlick. C-o-w-l-i-c-k."

Grace nodded.

Miss Lee smiled at Posey. "Grace was trying to say that you have

the same little swirl in your hair as
she does. Look."

Miss Lee took a small mirror
out of her desk drawer. She held it
up so Posey could see.

"This is a cowlick, right here."
Miss Lee pointed to the little swirl
near Posey's

part.

"I have one, too. See?" she said.

Miss Lee's cowlick was on the back of her head. Like Grace's.

"Cows don't have lips, do they?" said Miss Lee.

Posey shook her head. Grace did, too.

"Can you imagine cows wearing lipstick?" Miss Lee teased.

A cow wearing lipstick. It was such a silly idea.

Miss Lee pushed out her lips. She made a funny face. "MooOOOO," she said.

Miss Lee's cow sounded so real!

Posey giggled.

So did Grace.

"That's better." Miss Lee put the mirror back in her drawer. "I think we better write *cowlick* on the word wall, don't you?"

THE SAME BOOKS
POSEY READS

At the end of the day, Miss Lee clapped.

"Remember to have your reading slips signed tonight, everyone," she called. "I'm going to assign new reading partners tomorrow."

New reading partners! Maybe this time, Posey would get Ava or Nikki.

"If you don't have a book to take home, hurry and get one now," Miss Lee said.

Posey stood up to pick out a new book.

Grace stood up, too.

"Grace, you come with me." Miss Lee came over to their table and held out her hand. "You will pick from the books with the green dots."

Posey's eyes got very big. Grace
was in the bottom group.
"I want to read the
same books Posey
reads," said Grace.

Miss Lee took Grace's hand. "All of the books in our room are good."

"But Posey's my friend," Grace said in a little voice.

"She can still be your friend," said Miss Lee. "Come on. We'll find a book you will love."

Posey quietly picked a new book and put it in her backpack.

She and Ava and Nikki were in the red group. Three peas in a pod. That made Posey happy.

But what about Grace?

Grace didn't sound happy.

She sounded lonely. Like a tiny, sad mouse.

A KIND TEACHER

When Posey got home, she had her snack. Then she went to her room to play school.

She put on her tutu and her veil.

She was Princess Posey, a kind teacher.

Posey's stuffed animals were lined up on the bed.

There was Roger the giraffe. And Kiki the tiger. And Hoppy the frog. And Poinky the pig.

Wah was a baby. She didn't go to school. Posey put her under the covers to take a nap.

Posey used her magic wand to point at her pretend word wall. "Does anyone know what a cowlick is?" she asked.

They talked about the word. None of her animals had one. Then Posey said it was time for reading.

The animals looked excited. They all loved to read.

"Roger and Hoppy and Poinky," Posey said in her teacher voice, "you will read a book with a red dot."

She put the three animals together. She propped up a book in front of them.

Posey put her tiger at the end of the bed. "Kiki, you will read a book with a green dot," she said. She gave her a book, too.

"There," said Posey. "Now, everyone read."

She stood back. Something was wrong.

Kiki looked sad.

Posey crouched down so she could talk to her in a quiet voice.

"You will like the book with the green dot," she said. "All of the books in our room are good."

Kiki looked at her with sad brown eyes.

Looking at them made Posey sad, too.

She knew exactly how Kiki felt. She felt left out.

Posey stood up. "You want to read with a friend, don't you?" she said to Kiki.

Yes! Yes! Kiki was so excited.

Posey picked up Roger and put him next to Kiki.

"There," Posey

said. "You two can be reading partners."

Kiki thought it was the most
amazing thing. Her eyes sparkled
like stars. Roger looked happy,
too.

Now Posey knew how she could
help Grace feel better.

MAGIC LAND,
AT LAST

"**H**i, Miss Lee," Posey said the next morning.

Miss Lee looked up from her desk. "You're bright and early today, Posey," she said.

"Can Grace be my reading partner?" Posey asked.

"I think Grace would like that very much," said Miss Lee. "But what about you?"

"I want to," Posey said. "She's my friend."

"I'm glad." Miss Lee smiled. "Okay, then, you and Grace are reading partners for the next month. How's that?"

"Good."

Grace was so excited. When it was reading time, she and Posey took their books to the reading corner.

They sat side by side on the red and blue pillow.

"This is my favorite pillow," Grace said.

"Me too," said Posey.

It was so much fun to read together. When Grace didn't know a word, Posey helped her. It made Posey feel proud.

Before they knew it, it was time to go outside.

"Let's get Ava and Nikki," Posey said. "I have the most amazing game we can play."

The girls ran to the playground.

"I made up a new magic game," Posey told them. "It needs four people."

"That's how many we have," said Nikki.

"We're four peas in a pod!" Posey said.

"How do you play?" said Ava.

Posey told them about Magic Land.

"I want to be the giant," Nikki cried. She made mean giant growling noises.

"Can I be the unicorn, please, please?" Ava begged. "Unicorns are so special."

That left the princess and the lion.

Posey looked at Grace. "You can be the princess if you want."

"You have to be the princess," said Grace. "I want to be the lion who protects you!"

Grace gave a mighty roar. She sounded like a real lion.

"Let's go play!" Posey cried.

The unicorn, the giant, the lion, and the princess ran to play Magic Land.

This time, the princess let the lion hold her hand.

Watch for the next **PRINCESS POSEY** book!

PRINCESS P❀SEY
and the
CHRISTMAS MAGIC

Posey is sure Santa will bring her a real magic wand for Christmas—it will help her do so many wonderful things! But when an accident leads to a little white lie, she worries Santa won't come at all. Will Princess Posey's sparkly tutu help her find the courage to fix things?